IT HAPPENED AT CHURCH

IT HAPPENED AT CHURCH

By: N. Denise

*This book is dedicated to Denise Adams...
gone too soon.*

Table of Contents

I

New Year's Hoppin' John

My name is Vista Ann Settles, and I have been in church all my life! You see, I was born to a family of men and women preachers. My family tree is full of preachers after preachers. If a preacher is missing on a branch of my family tree, you are sure to find a deacon, deaconess, trustee, or usher. My family has played a role in all facets of church life and church business.

Now, I know I shouldn't tell everything I know, and I won't, but I thought it would make a good series to talk about all the "stuff" that happens at church. You know what I mean ... the things that happen that most folk new to "church" would never expect. I hope that people will see several things: church folk, old church folk, and young church folk are people too! Yes, we all are people subject to mistakes and shortfalls, but have I seen some big ones ... right in the church!

Now, I want you to recall in your church all the preparation that takes place for various church functions, especially those functions where the church is sure to draw visitors. You know the functions like Homecoming, a church anniversary, Women's day, Mothers' day, or Fathers' day. Many hands make work light unless you get a bunch of hands that want to be in charge. Look out!

Well, I want to tell you about the events leading up to the Watch-night service and the preparation to serve an old southern favorite: Hoppin John, collard greens, and cornbread! Now, this is an old tradition in my church, starting way back since I can remember thinking! We use to only have Hoppin John and greens. Cornbread was something our pastor wanted to add to the menu, so we went with it! After all, he is the man in charge!

Now, some of us—"seasoned" church folks—have done this, for many years, and we have a way to get everything done with no problem. Truth be told, there is always one fool in our bunch who has to cause some type of trouble. That is when I let loose, and while I know I shouldn't, well … I do it so that maybe for the next event, they will get an idea to leave me alone and stop the foolishness. But it never works, and the same nonsense happens each year.

During our regular meeting to prepare for the crowd that would be joining the church at New Year, everyone knew their role. Sister Bernetha would go to the food warehouse, along with me and Brother Joe. Brother Joe would usually drive, but this year, his daughter, Joanna, was the driver because Brother Joe was having problems with gout. He eats too much lunch meat if you ask me. It's strange because his wife swears that she cooks dinner every night except for Saturday, the day she takes "off" and wants to rest. I guess he is fixing those lunch meat sandwiches like that Dagwood character in the comic strip for lunch!

The rest of our kitchen team consisted of Sister Nell, Sister Pam, and Brother Nicholas. For Brother Nicholas, we like to call Saint Nick on a count that he always stays clear of the fights in the kitchen and usually he can even break them up! Now, Sisters Nell and Pam usually take on the task of decorating and assisting with the food if needed. I don't need help making this small menu, but every darn year; here, they come trying to put their foot in the pot. Brother Nicholas is there to help with cleanup and heavy lifting alongside Brother Joe. These men don't need to help us with the food except to taste it to make sure it's right!

Now, we all met at the church on Thursday morning since New Year's Day was Friday night. We piled into Brother Joe's truck with Joanna at the wheel, and off we went to the food warehouse. Joanna has a heavy foot when it comes to driving, and I knew once we stopped at the food warehouse, I would need to check my drawers because I was sho—. I sprinkled a little pee! Sister Bernetha must have pinched me one thousand times on the way there as Joanna stopped hard and turned even harder! It was like riding a roller coaster! But we were grateful for the ride so that we can keep things rolling right along.

When we were inside the food warehouse, we split up and picked up the black-eyed peas, rice, cornbread, and greens. It took forever to find the box of pork we use for the peas and greens. They moved them clear to the opposite side of the warehouse! Well, I was glad we found them, and the hocks looked and smelled just right!

We got back to the church with all of the ingredients and went about our business of storing them away and pulling pots and pans so that when we returned on Friday, all we needed to do was get to work. Now, we've been doing this for years, so we knew what we needed to do, and we did it.

Well, Sister Tidewater came. This woman is always trouble. She smells like trouble; she looks like trouble, and if you ask me, her middle name is Trouble! When she came to the church, she said she had a "Christian" experience. Well, she has some experience all right, with those tight suits she likes to wear ... always got the deacons looking and sweating when she walks by waving with that crooked smile!

So, as I said, she came into the kitchen as we were putting the purchases away and made a suggestion. Well, who asked her to give a suggestion? She needs to mind her damn business ...excuse me. See, I slip sometimes. She needs to mind her business.

"I think it would make your work easier if you make

the cornbread today and then refrigerate it until tomorrow. If you like, I can make it so y'all can rest up. What y'all think?" she said flashing that crooked smile at us.

I think Sister Bernetha's dentures slipped as she gave Sister Tidewater the "side-eye" and said kindly and sharply, "No, thank you. We have everything under control as we do every year we do this."

I said, "You know we always appreciate input from the members; however, we got this under control as Sister Bernetha has said. Besides, we want to make sure that the cornbread is made just the way the pastor likes it." I kept a half smile on my face in order to hopefully hide the sour taste in my mouth I had for Sister Tidewater.

She did not want to take no for an answer. She switched her weight to her left side and said, "Well, now, one day, y'all aren't going to be able to do this work. While it is nothing like the homecoming meals that are prepared, I would think you would appreciate another set of hands to help. Clearly, I was mistaken. I would really like to help, but if y'all don't want the help, just remember I offered."

Poor Brother Joe was frozen between the women. He looked at us and then back at Sister Tidewater, cleared his throat, and said, "Well, we are already finished putting everything away. It'd be a shame to pull it all out and start cooking when we did not plan to. Sister Tidewater, thank you for offering to help today, but if you really want to help us, please come back tomorrow afternoon. I am sure we can use your able hands then."

Sister Bernetha and I nodded in agreement. I was secretly hoping she would find something else to do because I don't think I could stand another know-it-all in the kitchen. She makes me sick! I try hard to do the right thing, but that woman is a mess. What does she want in this kitchen when what we are preparing won't take an army to put together?

"Oh, I see! That would probably be so much better for me," Sister Tidewater said, now standing upright. "I guess I will see you all tomorrow. What time should I be here? I want to make sure I put in my fair share of time!"

"Sister Bernetha likes to be here early afternoon so that the hocks and greens can be done early. I will bring the beans I soak at home in the early afternoon to cook here in the kitchen. So, if you want to arrive around two in the afternoon, that should be fine," I said.

"Well, I will be sure to come at two sharp, ready to show y'all my skills in the kitchen," Sister Tidewater said.

"Alright then, take care," Brother Nicholas said.

"I will, Brother Nicholas, and you tell your wife I said hello, now, ok?"

"I will, Sister Tidewater. I will."

"Bye," Sister Bernetha and I said simultaneously before going back to what we were doing.

On Friday morning, I had all the beans cleaned, sorted, and already soaked overnight. See, you can't be playing when you cooking for a crowd of mixed company! If someone gets a stone or an uncooked bean, the word will spread faster than venereal disease did in the '60s! To add insult to injury, they would be sure to say it was my job to make sure the quality was right. I think they call that something like quality assurance or something! Well, if that was my job, you better believe I was gonna do it right!

I got to the church just around eleven in the morning. Saint Nick was in there putting the water in the big pot for the hock to cook while I went for the pots I needed to make the rice and the peas. Just after I arrived, Sister Bernetha came in.

"I hope that Sister Tidewater stays home," she hissed. "I cannot for the life of me think of why she wants to be in here anyway! I am sure she has something better to do today!"

"Well, if she comes, keep her to one task—the cornbread! If we mix that before she comes, she can just pour it into the pans and keep watch while it bakes," I added.

There was not much more talk of that woman as we went on with our tasks. We spent time talking about the Sunday sermon that was delivered by the assistant pastor, Dr. Brave. We all like her; we like the pastor too, but this young woman delivers the word with a punch! We talked about other not-so-churchy stuff, like the fight at a funeral the week before. I must tell you all about that another time, but it was nasty!

Sister Tidewater never made it in ... until later that evening. We were all in the kitchen, and just as Sister Bernetha was preparing to cut up the cornbread, Sister Tidewater walked in shaking her finger, saying, "Don't touch that cornbread! I am here to help!"

The whole kitchen stood still as I, Brother Joe, and Saint Nick held our breath praying Sister Bernetha did not use the knife a different way!

Sisters Pam and Nell tipped to the doorway to see what the yelling was about.

"Everything alright in here?" Pam asked nervously while looking at Sister Tidewater.

"We heard Sister Tidewater yell, and we came to make sure everything was alright," Sister Nell said while nervously looking at Sister Bernetha holding the knife and Sister Tidewater.

"Oh, everything is alright now that I am here! Sister Bernetha was just about to cut that cornbread, and I wanted to make sure she left it for me to do," Sister Tidewater said smiling and tying an apron over her hot red-colored suit.

Who would wear a hot red suit to watch-night service!?

"Well, now as I recall, we told you we did not need help. However, if we were to use you, Saint, I mean, Brother Nicholas told you to come earlier today. You were not here, and then I am not sure why you are here ..."

"Oh, Sister Tidewater," Brother Nicholas interrupted Sister Bernetha. "We sure are glad you are here! While we have the food under control, I am sure Sisters Pam and Nell could give you a task as the people come in to eat. We always like it when the flow of people is smooth and moving."

Sister Bernetha gave Saint Nicholas a look that said he saved a life just before the New Year came in. I am always amazed at how that man can turn things around! Thank God he can because I knew the next words from Sister Bernetha were surely going to be some cuss words!

Now, at this point, Sister Tidewater had taken in what Sister Bernetha said up until she was interrupted, and she was clearly not going to let that stop her from saying, "Well, Sister Bernetha, I was not able to be here earlier on a count of my family being at my home a little longer than I anticipated. I am sure you know how that can be. Anyway, that cornbread looks a little dry, and I surely don't want to be associated with dry cornbread. I will take Brother Nicholas' suggestion and assist the people coming in for a meal. Maybe I can warn them to be sure to get a beverage before they eat the cornbread. Happy New Year everyone!" she sneered as she sashayed out of the kitchen with Sisters Pam and Nell.

"Jezebel," Sister Bernetha hissed and took a step toward the doorway of the kitchen.

I touched Sister Bernetha's arm and said, "Girl, you know she isn't worth the fight, and we need that knife to cut this cornbread. It is hardly dry. That woman is messy and will do anything to get a rise out of folk. She knows in here, in church, nobody gonna touch her. Well, maybe she is wrong about that, but I surely am not about to let you mess up that knife on a count of her nonsense!"

"That is some good cornbread. That woman hardly cooks to know the difference between what is bad and good," Brother Joe added.

After a moment or two, Sister Bernetha went back to the task of cutting up those pans of cornbread. I was happy I was not going to have to call the law! Sister Bernetha is no stranger to scrapping, and while it has surely been a while since the notorious "Kitchen Brawl," I surely don't want a repeat.

The Notorious Kitchen Brawl took place years ago when Sister Bernetha was a younger woman in her twenties. There was another young member, about the same age, who did not like Sister Bernetha since they were just girls in school. They said it had something to do with a boy ... but no one was clear about that. Now, this young woman would not stay out of the kitchen when Sister Bernetha was in there. Sister Bernetha at that time was there helping with desserts, cutting, and putting them on plates. Well, this woman came in, shaking her finger in Sister Bernetha's face about this same boy, who was now a man. The woman accused Sister Bernetha of something sinister. I mean sinister and nasty, and the next thing we know, a sweet potato pie went flying into that woman's face! Sister Bernetha was right behind that pie with a knife and a spatula! We all scattered to get to safety because that fight was on! While Sister Bernetha only skinned the woman a little, it took prayer and restraint to avoid calling the police! That woman was upset that her trash-talking got her beaten, and she wanted her abuser arrested. Well, Rev. Dr. Ben Jonathan Worthy, our pastor, came in there and prayed while First Lady Laney Worthy—a nurse—cleaned the wounds. After the prayer, those two ladies had to follow him to his office with First Lady Worthy and two Deaconesses. Whatever happened behind those doors worked because, from that point on, Sister Bernetha and that woman never had words again. That young woman left the church to follow a man some years back, and she is still marked up from that fight.

The kitchen was a mess after that brawl! We had a ton of folks wondering if there was some type of accident, and we let them go right on believing that is just what happened. No need for visitors to know the messy side of our "church" business.

Now, Sister Tidewater may not know about The Notorious Kitchen Brawl, because if she did, she would not have said what she said. Sister Bernetha was holding that knife just ready. I could see it in her eyes. Folk just don't know what a person has been through! Leave folks alone!

Just before the benediction into the New Year, we were all ready and set up to start feeding the people who would be coming down from service. Sister Tidewater positioned herself at the doorway to the dining room so she could direct traffic. I only prayed she would not tell that lie about the cornbread being dry! The people started coming first in trickles, those we will not see again until the end of the year. They try to get their food before everyone else. They even try to get an extra plate to go for the heathens that would not get up or stop partying to come to church!

Sisters Pam and Nell were making sure Bishop Horace T. Jennings' dining room was ready. After they were sure everything was in order, they joined Sister Tidewater at the doors to help guide the flow of people into the room and to the kitchen window.

The food was going to be passed through the kitchen window this year. This was different from past years because we did not want to set up a serving table. We could keep the food hot and make the plates right there. We have a nice setup, and we used it to our advantage.

Now that the bulk of the worshippers was now in the dining room, we were in full serving mode. Everyone ranted and raved about how nice the room was decorated. No complaints about the food from the key people, like the pastor and first lady. All my family said they were very satisfied; after all, this was not a full-fledged dinner ... it was just a quick bite after entering the New Year.

So, someone should tell me why in the world did Sister Tidewater come out with her face saying that we need to consider making a dinner next year with to-go plates and all? The crowd never last longer than it takes to eat that small plate. So, while we were cleaning up and preparing to head home, Sister Tidewater came in with that suggestion. No one answered her.

Just then, the pastor came in alongside his first lady and thanked us for making the meal. He even commented on the cornbread being just what he loved as a young boy.

Sister Tidewater chimed in with her comment, "Pastor, wouldn't you be even happier leaving the church with a full belly? What I mean is maybe we could do a full dinner next year. That way, if people want to take food home, they can, and the rest can stay here and enjoy a good ole southern meal before they leave."

The pastor who was never one to shy away from anything, simply said, "No. I believe that my members, who are here right now, are doing a fine job with the New Year menu. If there are any changes, I am sure they will let me know their idea at the appropriate time, and at that time, we can discuss them. Until then, this wheel is not squeaking, and there is no need for oil. First Lady, I do believe we need to head home. Thank you everyone again for doing such a fine job!"

And with that, the pastor and his first lady left the kitchen. Sister Tidewater was clearly taken aback that she did not have the last word, and I am sure she was even more surprised that the pastor did not entertain her suggestion.

After, a few moments, we went right back to the last details of cleaning up and closing the kitchen. Sister

Tidewater was just standing there like she needed the invitation to help ... or maybe she was overseeing what we were doing. Just then, as we were locking the refrigerator, Sister Tidewater had one last thing to say.

"Well, I suppose the pastor was just being nice regarding the cornbread. I still think it was too dry. But that may be what brings back such fond childhood memories for the pastor."

Just then, I knew we all needed to keep an eye on Sister Bernetha. I moved toward Sister Tidewater and asked her if she needed something because we are done and don't need another hand. But Sister Bernetha started walking really slowly toward Sister Tidewater.

"Listen to me one more time; when I tell you we don't need help in here, I mean it! And that means we don't need your stanking opinions or your criticism. Now, keep on pushing that button and you gonna get the prize!" Just before Sister Bernetha reached Sister Tidewater, Brother Joe stepped between them.

At that point, Sister Tidewater must have finally understood that she was truly barking up the wrong tree. Without another word, she turned and left the kitchen, and she even left the church building. Now, it took a moment for us to calm down and calm Sister Bernetha. We ended the night with prayer, as usual, and asked God to help us remain patient when pie burns ... that means pushed to the limit.

2

African American Food Tasting (Black History Month)

It is Black History Month, and every year, it is such an exciting time at the church. We open the archives and share all the information from the generations of people who form the foundation of this branch of Zion. I especially love when we pull out the old songs ... "spirituals" they call them. When the oldest member gets a hold of that microphone and all you can hear is the rich, deep, soulful, love, and history of the African American, that makes you want to shout! One year, my wig was loose after shouting up and down the aisle. When the Spirit let me go, the usher had to give me a hairpin and a mirror.

On Black History Month, we serve two dinners: one for the African American Food Tasting and Discussion, and the other, we serve on the last Sunday of February to close out Black History Month. For these two dinners, we have some regular members who always assist us in the kitchen as a part of the Stewards' Ministry. Now, your church might call it something else; in my sister's church, they call it the Culinary Ministry. I guess maybe there is a chef in the ministry ... I like the name "Culinary Ministry" better. But no matter what the name is—Steward or Culinary—it is the Ministry where the folks cook the food! We sure can make things difficult with titles and names!

Now, as I was saying, there are more people to help in the kitchen since this is a big meal. The first dinner is for the African American Food Tasting and Discussion. The whole idea is that people would bring a dish to share with the group so that we can all enjoy something from a different region of the world or just different regions of the United States. The discussion would center on whatever the Black History Committee decides. Last year, we talked about the number of people who have graduated from high school and how to get those numbers to be 100 percent. We talked about what makes young people drop out and how we can help them avoid that decision and circumstance. What makes this event different is that First Lady Worthy decided that the Steward Ministry would provide some of the food so that we can avoid having situations where there is too much starch, no vegetables, or no meat. In January, we ask those who are interested in sharing a dish to sign up with the First Lady. People always seem to move faster when they are sort of reporting to the First Lady. Before February, we knew what to expect. The Church secretary confirms with the participants the dish they plan to bring. In the past, The Butler Sisters signed up to bring jerk chicken and roti. I sure had my mouth tuned up for that dish, only to learn that the sisters had a slight miscommunication as to who was doing the chicken and who was doing the roti! So, we ended up with rotis! Well, we all laughed at that later! The Butler Sisters are something else!

With the list and confirmation, the Stewards now knew what we needed to do to keep things a little balanced. This year was no different.   We already did the shopping, and our assignments were made. If I did not tell you before now, when you get your assignment, you don't go poking your nose in anyone else's assignment. Prepare the food you were assigned to prepare. If you prefer less pepper in your beans, and someone else cooking puts more in than you like, you just have to roll with the punches. Maybe go home and make your own beans. Just stay in your lane, as the young people say, and complete what you were assigned to do. If someone asks for your opinion, well, that is something else.

Saturday, the day before the African American Food Tasting and Discussion, we were all gathered in the kitchen to start the prep work. The plan was laid out that all the chopping and seasoning would be done the day before, and we would all come back to cook it on Sunday morning. The

Gospel music was playing in the multipurpose room while most of us hummed and others bantered about subjects. I love these sounds of love and working together with no drama. The so-called prep day went on without a problem!

Sunday morning came early for me! I was at the church just as the trustee was unlocking the doors at 5 am. Yes, I love to get in that kitchen and fire up the ovens, not too hot, just at 325 degrees to get started. I went about my business and started pulling out the items I was assigned as well as Sister Bernetha's items. We work together in that respect; if she gets here before me, she pulls my food out. Today, I beat her in!

I was given the task of making cabbage, and what I call "Dirty Rice." Dirty Rice is that rice we throw some shrimp and sausage in along with green onions, and sometimes, a little carrot and egg. I was not doing carrots and eggs this time. The shrimp was seasoned the night before, so all I really needed to do was steam the rice, jasmine rice for the fragrance, and cook the sausage. I like to use two spicy sausage rolls and two sage-spiced sausage rolls. It gives the rice a balance, and hopefully, people who cannot handle spicy foods will be able to eat it. The cabbage was already made the night before and needed to be reheated.

Shortly after I started making my food, Sister Bernetha came in. She seemed in good spirits with a smile on her face.

"Good morning, 'Netha! You look like the cat that swallowed the canary!" I said laughing.

"Well, if that is so, that canary was delicious to me!" Bernetha said laughing.

"What made you so tickled this morning? Or is this just what those young people say is a natural high."

Bernetha looked at me as she was pulling her food together and said, "It's all-natural. I just woke up feeling good, like I could take on the world. So, I am praying nothing causes that to change. You know how it is in this kitchen!"

"Yes, I sure do!" We went right into our routine of preparing the food we were asked to prepare. Not long after we stopped giggling, the rest of the folks came in to do their parts.

As you already know, there is always one person who wants to show up at the last minute, and when they do, it could cause a huge mess of trouble. Last time, it was Sister Tidewater, and here, she was again! She sashayed into the kitchen just before the African American Food Tasting began to lend her hand.

"Well, good afternoon good people! I am here to be an extra set of hands wherever you need me," she exclaimed. Sister Bernetha never looked up from what she was doing. I kept an eye on her and Sister Tidewater just to make sure they did not cross paths.

When no one spoke up, Brother Joe said, "Hello sister, I believe we have everything under control in the kitchen. What I am almost sure we need are people to help us label dishes and place them on the table so that people can serve themselves."

"Oh, I can certainly do that. Are there any premade cards or should I write them out myself?" Sister Tidewater said as she moved toward the desk to the side of the kitchen.

"They are premade, so all you need to do is make sure they are placed properly with the dish. The First Lady will also be here to make sure the table is set up properly," Brother Joe said as he showed Sister Tidewater where the cards were.

"Thank you, Brother Joe! I knew you were the one to talk to. I would do better at this anyway. Organizing is what I do best. I will leave the kitchen to you, able-bodied folks!" Sister Tidewater said as she turned to leave the kitchen.

The kitchen was silent again until Sister Bernetha, who did not seem to be paying attention to the conversation began humming *Jesus is real to me* just loud enough for us to hear it and join in. It was nice the way that happened. Just as we completed the last round, we were ready to bring the food out.

The First Lady, also known as Sister Laney, came in ready to serve! She was never one to shy away from getting her hands dirty. I mean that literally too. One year, just after our church received a grant to start a garden, she was right there planting greens, tomatoes, cucumbers, radishes, and anything else she knew would be abundant enough to share with the community. When it was time to harvest what grew, she was there before everyone else with two already-filled big shopping bags with vegetables! First Lady Laney is a wonderful, humble woman. She is not someone who likes foolishness and disruption, and she is known to take care of it on the spot.

I recall a time when we had a function at the church. I believe it was World Aids Day or something along those lines. The speaker was talking to us about what we can do to help those with HIV. Well, some bigoted body stood up and declared that we should not be helping heathens and nasty gay men because the Lord was dealing with them and that is why they have HIV. Well, First Lady Laney raised her hand as if to bring a hush over the crowd, stood up, and took the podium. After giving the speaker a reassuring look, she faced the audience and said, "Ye without sin, cast the first stone. Seeing as no one here is sin-free, how dare any of us decide that we will not help another human being in need? HIV is not a gay man's disease, as was stated earlier in this gathering. HIV is affecting everyone from every walk of life and every sexual preference. Now, in this space, we are here to do God's work. If you are here on behalf of the enemy to do his work, you may leave, and we will pray for you, and you are welcome to return anytime you decide that you are a part of God's team." No one left, and as she gave the podium back to the speaker, there was a round of applause. The man that yelled that comment even apologized to the First Lady. He wanted to take the mic and apologize, but she discouraged him from doing that. The program went on as if nothing happened. From then on, it was never a good idea to cross the First Lady. But some tried without even knowing how she operates. I will tell you about that later.

With her hat safely stored in the closet, the First Lady placed her suit jacket on a hanger, put on her apron, and began to organize the serving table. Sister Tidewater came over to make sure she was "seen" by the First Lady. The ladies who were helping First Lady took direction from her, and the table was set up very pretty and neatly. The food was organized so that the hot foods were on one end and the cold items were on the opposite end, as they should be.

The room was near capacity with just about every table full before the program started. Pastor Worthy and First Lady Worthy, who at that time was already fully dressed, came in and took their seats after greeting several guests along the way.

The program went on without a hitch. Well, that is until Sister Tidewater made it her business during the discussion part of the "Tasting" to take a phone away from one of our guests as it lay on the table while he was distracted. The guest was none other than Rev. Kanklon, who had a large congregation on the other side of town. His church suffered an efflux of members when a scandal broke out in the news about the previous pastor. That story I have to tell you about later. Rev. Kanklon came to our church hoping to get some ideas to take back to his congregation. His church was just getting back to normal. His congregation often attended our functions, as we sometimes reciprocate.

"I seem to have misplaced my phone," Rev. Kanklon said looking around the table and then looking at the ground.

"Is that so? Let me help you look for it. These days, we need those phones to keep things in order!" Pastor Worthy said. Both men started looking for the phone, as others around them did the same.

When the tasting was over, the multipurpose room began to thin out. Just as they were going to give up looking, Sister Tidewater walked up looking smug.

"Hello, Pastor Worthy; First Lady. Before I left for the evening, I thought I better make sure this young man gets his phone back. Here you go, and let this be a lesson to you that when there is a program taking place, it would be best that you pay attention to the speaker than what is happening on your phone." Sister Tidewater took a motherly stance as if to say "you better remember what I said or else."

As Rev. Kanklon took the phone, he looked at Pastor Worthy with amazement. He then turned to Sister Tidewater and said, "I don't think we have met. My name is Rev. Kanklon. I am the pastor of First Baptist Church. While I am not one to ever explain myself, allow me to offer you this information: I take notes with this phone ... electronic notes so that I never need paper which can be misplaced. I am not sure what your motivation was, but I think it would have served you better to have taken a moment to simply ask me what I was doing before taking a position of authority over a grown man and taking his phone without permission."

"Oh. Oh. I um ... I did not realize who you were. I am so embarrassed ... I am so— I apologize, Rev. Kanklon. I certainly didn't ..." Sister Tidewater stumbled over her words, and no one tried to help.

Finally, after a few more stuttered words from Sister Tidewater, First Lady Laney interrupted.

"Rev. Kanklon, thank you for being here! I am very pleased you have your phone back! Pastor Worthy and I would have been happy to replace it! Thankfully, the mystery is solved. Let me know if you missed any part of the program for your notes, and I will get them to you right away!"

"Thank you, First Lady! Pastor Worthy, please check your calendar for the day you might be free for a round of golf! I need a chance to redeem myself!" Rev. Kanklon said while extending his hand to Pastor Worthy.

"You will never be able to do that! I have my golf game all wrapped up!" Pastor Worthy laughed as he and Rev. Kanklon headed for the door, leaving the ladies.

"Sister Tidewater, allow me to share a bit of wisdom with you," First Lady Laney started. "You will never know every person who attends our functions here. There have always been people from different cultures, religions, backgrounds, and experiences coming here. I, like Rev.

Kanklon, am not sure what your motivation was. What you did this evening was childish, and quite frankly, it is none of your business what that man was doing. Please, control your temptation to correct anyone you don't know. This could have very well gone in a different direction. Good night, and do drive carefully." After she finished, First Lady Laney, without waiting for a response, made her way to the parking lot to meet her husband.

Now, y'all probably wonder how I could stand in the distance and not be noticed. That is my job. I think my friend called me "Cat feet" because I am rarely heard entering or leaving a room. It takes talent to do that, and I am not sure if that is a talent left over from my childhood or some other life. Now, let me tell you, I was not the only person standing there because usually, it is me and Sister Bernetha who ride together. This evening, we planned to be the last to leave the multipurpose room so we can turn out the lights. We came to the doorway of the kitchen just as this scene was unfolding. That woman, Sister Tidewater is truly a mess!

3

The Funeral

Before the end of February, there was a funeral planned for a man named Jewelz Mason. He was the son of one of the past ministers at our church. We all loved Jewelz. He was obedient, quiet, and reliable. His parents held him a little higher than the other three children they had. You see, Rev. Mason always thought he could tell where a child was going in life. He felt Jewelz was going to follow in his footsteps and become a minister. Well, that sure didn't happen!!

Jewelz was very smart and completed his studies to become an engineer. After college, he went on to the military for a while and resigned from his commission as a Captain. We were all very proud of him. Somewhere after that, Jewelz started being a big ladies' man. Maybe he was one all along, but now, there was a wife and children involved.

The story his Mom told me was like something out of the movies. Jewelz married a wonderful lady, Mesalyn with whom he had two sons. While Mesalyn was pregnant with baby number three, which turned out to be twin girls, Jewelz started seeing another woman. Now, this lady was nice enough except she was messing with a married man! Her name was Dion, and she had a son named Deon. Dion was also very married to Scott who was out of town often for work.

His sons did not know that he was fooling around with their friend's mom, Dion. The way they found out was a mess itself! The boys—ages 17 and 16—were all out at a party. Mesalyn gave her sons, Jason and Zach, permission to sleep over at Dion's house with her son Deon. Oh, did I forget to tell you that Dion and Mesalyn knew each other through their sons? Yes, they knew one another from all the sports and social functions surrounding the sports the boys' played.

Let me make sure you follow this story: Jewelz and Mesalyn are married with two boys, Jason and Zach. Dion is the lover to Jewelz, and she has a son named Deon and is married to Scott.

Now, the boys were at this party, and when it ended, the boys went to Dion's house. When they got there, the house was quiet and dark, no surprise. The surprise was Jewelz did not time it right and came out of Dion's room as the boys were heading into the room they were to sleep in!

Well, they were no fools, but Jewelz attempted to tell them that he was just checking on Dion, but Dion came out half naked, and the story Jewelz was telling fell apart. Poor Scott was out of town.

Now, those boys adore their momma, and Zach planned to tell his mom as soon as he got home. Well, Jason called his mom right away, but Zach got him to hang up. Jewelz asked them to look away and not tell anyone, and in exchange, he would stop seeing Dion. But everyone was so busy trying to keep it from Mesalyn that they forgot Deon was there! So, you know, he called Mesalyn that next morning and told her that Jewelz was at his house the night before. Mesalyn, no stranger to Jewelz messing around, was calm and thanked Deon.

Several months passed, and unknown to anyone else, Mesalyn hired a private investigator and put one of those things on Jewelz's car to know where he went to. The results were upsetting enough to send Mesalyn into early labor! The girls were born with no real issues, and the family surrounded them with love.

When they got those babies home, Mesalyn asked Jewelz to leave the home they custom-built. Jewelz acted surprised, and before he knew it, Mesalyn's brothers came from the back room with an envelope full of pictures and information detailing his infidelity. Jewelz was fooling around with Dion and other women!

Jewelz was hurt that he was caught and had asked his

wife for forgiveness. Mesalyn was not moved, but she said she would consider his apology after he moved out. Jewelz moved out to his parent's estate and was there for several months before moving in with one of his mistresses! His parents were furious, but what could they do? Jewelz stayed with this woman for three years before he had a heart attack. His mistress, Destiny called 911 after finding him on the floor not responding to her screaming at him. The 911 folks came, got him, and took him to the hospital. And there he was laid up in ICU.

You would think that the mistress, although living with Jewelz, who was still married, would try not to make a scene. Well, when Mesalyn showed up with the girls to see how Jewelz was doing, Destiny went crazy! The Plafker waiting room became a loud screaming arena with the headliner being Destiny! She cussed and screamed something awful! So much so that Rev. and Mrs. Mason froze in disgust and surprise. Jason and Zach were standing in front of their mom, and the twins ran to their grandparents. It was ugly! When security showed up, Destiny actually thought she had a say in who could see "her man." That was when a very calm Mesalyn said, "I want to check on him for myself with my sons, and if they will allow, I want my girls to see their dad. If the diagnosis is as bad as Mrs. Mason has told me, this could be the last time they see their father."

The security guard was nice to Mesalyn, and he told her that unless she was family, she really could not go in.

When she learned that Mesalyn was still married to Jewelz and that Destiny was the mistress, she quickly changed her mood toward Destiny.

"Miss, you don't have any right to tell this man's wife or his children that they cannot see him. Unless you have some type of document like a restraining order or Medical Power of Attorney, you are just a visitor to this family. If I were you, I would not be here making any more scenes, or we will escort you out of here, and you will not be coming back onto this hospital campus unless you are a patient. Am I making myself clear?" The security guard glared at Destiny as if to say "I dare you." Destiny shook her head "yes" after looking around the room to see if there was anyone who could help her.

Mesalyn was escorted into the room by her now-grown sons. They were tall and handsome like their father. Both young men were doing well, and they still loved their mom like before. Both remained supportive of their mom and never gave Destiny the attention she wanted from them. They remained respectful to Destiny, but beyond that, she was one of the reasons their parents split.

When Mesalyn, Jason, and Zach entered the room, Mesalyn stopped at the doorway while the young men went to their dad's side. She could see that he seemed to have aged since the last time she saw him. Mesalyn and Jewelz decided to steer clear of each other using his parent's estate as the drop-off and pick-up spot for the children. Most times, Mesalyn was gone before Jewelz could get there.

She went to the bedside and took his hand. His hand was cold and lifeless. His skin was ashy like he needed to use lotion or something. The boys were telling their dad that they were there, and Jason nudged his mom so she could talk to Jewelz too.

"'Welz, it's me, Mesalyn. I am here by your side. I hope you can hear me and the boys. The girls are in the waiting room with your parents. Can you squeeze my hand so I know you are ok?" Mesalyn waited, but there was nothing. A tear fell down her cheek. She continued to talk to him until she felt like she could get the girls, who were now 3 years old.

Mesalyn came out to the waiting room only to be met with Destiny asking her how long it was going to be before she completed her visit with the children so she could get back into Jewelz's room. Mesalyn ignored her and went to Rev. and Mrs. Mason. The look on her face said enough for Mrs. Mason to get up and hug Mesalyn. "Mesa, girl, stay strong! Jewelz is covered in prayer, and we will continue doing just that ... Praying! Try to stay strong for the children. Go! Take Jewel and Jewelz to see their father." Mrs. Mason was a gentlewoman, but don't let that fool you. She was just a moment away from telling Destiny where to go in Jesus' name!

Mesalyn explained to the girls that their dad was sleeping and was doing his best to get better. She told them to be good and use their inside voices. Both girls looked with concern at their mother but nodded that they understood.

When the nurse came into the waiting area, Mr. & Mrs. Mason were initially alarmed, along with Destiny. After explaining what she was there for, to tell them it appeared their son might wake up, the alarm was replaced with squeals of hope. But that gal Destiny was determined to be recognized in some important way. She stood up and demanded that Mesalyn come out so that she could be by Jewelz's side. The nurse looked at that girl with disgust and told her to wait there, and she would see what she could do. You see, word travels fast when there is a heifer like Destiny in the building! The staff is usually on the side of the family and will protect them at all costs!

Rev. and Mrs. Mason came into the room and were met with smiles and giggles. The twins were holding Jewelz right hand together saying they love him. Mrs. Mason took his left hand and spoke softly.

"Jewelz, this is your momma. Your daddy is right here. Boy, fight and get yourself well! We love you, son! You know we do, and we are praying that the Lord will heal you this day!"

Rev. Mason placed his hand on his wife's shoulder, and they stood there happy to see some life come back into their son.

Several days went by, according to Mrs. Mason. Each day, they prayed Jewelz would wake up. His skin was much better looking, and everything seemed to be going right.

A week to the day Destiny found Jewelz, he woke up. Destiny did not call the family for several hours. Destiny told the nurses his family knew he was awake and they were on the way. She lied so she could have him to herself. I told y'all she was a liar, but she is selfish too!

Rev. and Mrs. Mason always came to the hospital after a light lunch. That day was no different. When they arrived, the nurse commented that she was waiting for some time to see them. When Rev. Mason gave her a puzzled look, she explained that Jewelz was awake and communicating for several hours, and she thought they knew. Well, let me tell you, Rev. Mason stretched his eyes so wide, Mrs. Mason thought they would pop out! She tugged his arm and guided him to the room.

In the room, Destiny was holding Jewelz's hand and smiling in his face. When she saw the Masons, she immediately squealed in delight, "Oh my goodness! Look, your parents are here just in time to see you awake!"

Jewelz turned his head and smiled at his parents. Rev. Mason fell into Jewelz with a hug and laughter. Mrs. Mason took the opposite side where Destiny was, replacing her and taking her son's hand.

"Our prayers are answered! God is good and faithful! Jewelz, you are here, son. You are here!"

Destiny was now clutching her hands and standing at the foot of Jewelz's bed smiling. Jewelz was still connected to that machine to help him breathe but clearly was happy to see his parents. Mrs. Mason told Jewelz she would call the children and have them come right away. Destiny quickly volunteered that she would call.

Well, Rev. Mason cleared his throat, and with a deep and serious tone, he said, "Destiny, I believe we have been very patient and fair with you. However, we were mistaken when we thought we could trust you. My wife will contact our grandchildren and daughter-in-law to inform them of the change we are witnessing here in our son. I am not sure what your motives were in not contacting us about Jewelz waking up, and it is not really any concern of ours. What I will tell you is that you will not take the authority that we have in reaching our family. Thank you for offering, but we have our family covered."

Jewelz looked at Destiny with a puzzled look, but all she could do was look down and apologize.

The doctor came in excited to see his patient awake. He did a physical on Jewelz and posed some questions to him. Jewelz responded with a nod here and there. Eventually, the tube to his throat was removed, and after some coughing, Jewelz was able to speak.

With his raspy voice, Jewelz spoke to his mom first. "Hey, Momma! I love you more than ever! Dad, man, you are so awesome! Thank you for being here for me! I love you both so much."

"Son, we will be here until we die. You are our son. We

need you to get well and live a healthy life. Your family needs you to survive, son. We have prayed, and God has come through! You woke up! I cannot wait until the children see this," Rev. Mason said smiling and fist-pumping the air.

Just then, the door opened, and in came the four Mason children. Destiny went off to the side, looking helpless and guilty, and watched as the family showed love to their son and father. As she went to the door, she told Jewelz she would be right back to give them privacy. When she arrived in the waiting area, Mesalyn was there. Sitting with her was her brother Chase. Destiny just sighed and sat on the far end of the room from the siblings.

Mesalyn always brought her brother Chase along if she suspected there would be trouble. Chase was a tall, medium-built, but extremely fit and strong man. He was a private security guard for a certain well-known rap artist. He was known to be discreet. You would never see him coming if you were out of control. Usually, all he would need to do is stand up and look at you, like old-school Mommas did to get their children under control!

Mesalyn touched Chase's knee as if to say wait here. She went across the room to Destiny to ask how Jewelz was doing.

Destiny took a glance behind Mesalyn to see where Chase was and said, "My Jewelz is doing great! He woke up with me by his side and has been doing well. Why are you asking anyway? Why are you here anyway? He is divorcing you. You don't need to be here. He has me," Destiny hissed... but not too much as to draw Chase over to her side of the waiting area.

Mesalyn sighed and while never taking her eye off Destiny, said, "Destiny, I pose no threat to you or your relationship with Jewelz. The children that he and I have are what we now have in common. His choice was to be with someone I would hope makes him happy. I only want to see him happy. My reasons for being here are truly to support the family. If you took the time to see it, you would see that I am here to support you too. That is if you feel you are his family." Mesalyn walked away before Destiny could say anything.

As she reached Chase who was now standing, the children came out to meet their mom. The four of them were excited to tell Mesalyn that their dad was wide awake and talking. Mesalyn was happy to hear the news and waited for the Masons to come out. When they did, they did not go to Destiny, but to Mesalyn to provide her with the update. There was some other information they shared with her, but it was clear that it was for Mesalyn's ears only.

Destiny took that opportunity to head back into the room with Jewelz.

Jewelz was transferred out of ICU the next day and began getting some PT while waiting for a bed in rehab. He was strong, and he glowed in his face when Sister Bernetha and I went to see him. That was the last that we saw Jewelz alive.

Later that night, he started complaining of a headache. He said he thought it was from overdoing it in PT. He went to bed to rest. When the nurse came in a very short time later, he was unresponsive, and they had to call for help! They tried to revive him, but he did not make it. Sister Mason said it was an aneurysm in his head and that there was nothing they could do but let their son go. They said that while they figured out what happened, he was already gone in the brain ... brain dead is what they call it. The whole thing was a mess! But one person I can tell you that held it all together was Rev. and Sister Mason. I have never seen parents so strong in the face of the death of their child. Now, I have two boys and three girls, and while I pray I never have to bury any of them, one of my boys is truly a rowdy mess! If the Lord said guess which one I am gonna take, well let me say I would not be surprised if he took my rowdy boy! I have to tell you about my children another time.

So, now that Jewelz is passed on, the arrangements must be made. The local African American funeral home, Devanaux Home for Funerals was the choice for most families in this area. Destiny, for some reason, told the funeral home that her family uses Franklin Funeral Home and that they should come to collect the body! Well, there they were Devanaux and Franklin, sitting at the morgue trying to collect the same body!

Each funeral home called their living client trying to sort out this mess. Well, Franklin yielded to Devanaux after realizing that the check was with the Masons and not with Destiny! When I tell you it was a mess, well it was!

Destiny felt slighted, and the Masons just wanted a peaceful home going for their son. Destiny came to the estate of Rev. and Mrs. Mason only to find a large gathering of Masons including the estranged wife, Mesalyn. No one was rude to Destiny; however, it was clear that she would not have the same welcome as Mesalyn.

Destiny asked Rev. and Mrs. Mason if she could have a word with them. They welcomed her to the gazebo in the garden, hoping that being a few yards away from the house was fine and no one would notice. The Masons' oldest daughter, Jasmyn, came with them, as she had heard of this Destiny and her antics. She was not one to cross when it came to her family. She and Mesalyn were very close.

When they reached the gazebo, the ladies sat down while Rev. Mason stood next to his wife. Destiny wasted no time in making her plea to be a part of the planning for Jewelz's funeral.

Destiny asked, "I would like to be able to speak at the funeral, pick the flowers, and choose his casket and the suit he should wear. I would also like to take my place next to you, Mrs. Mason, in the front pew with the family. I realize that Jewelz and I did not marry, but it was his intention. We talked about getting married, but the time just ran out on us with his heart attack, and then the ... well, I was there through it all. I am not asking for too much, I hope. Jewelz was my world, and I loved him." Destiny started to cry, and as the tears fell, Rev. Mason offered his handkerchief. Destiny took it and dabbed her eyes.

"Well, I believe I can speak for my wife when I say I was not prepared for this conversation. Jewelz left us in a position that I never thought I would find us in. While it is true that you and Jewelz were certainly together, he has a wife and children who ..."

"Forget his wife ... she put him out of the house he built! She sent him into the street as if he was not a great husband and father to his family! If it was not for me, where would he live? Neither you nor your wife wanted him here, and it is clear you both are selfish! With all this space, why would you put your son out of this ... this ... mansion?" Destiny half screeched.

Jasmyn stood up and then sat back down as she needed to control her temper. Her parents had a house full of people, and this would not be a great time for her to slap her brother's grieving girlfriend!

"Destiny," Jasmyn said through gritted teeth. "You are here. On our estate ... our family estate. You are a welcome guest; however, that can change very fast. I am suggesting, with all the patience I can muster, that you lower your voice and get it together. Now, my brother is dead. We are all grieving, including his wife. My parents do not need additional stress with you acting like a wife when you were on rent! You seem puzzled and surprised. You ... were ... on ...rent!" After hearing where Jasmyn was going, Rev. and Mrs. Mason got up and without looking at Destiny went back into their home.

Jasmyn kept talking to a stunned Destiny.

"Now, let me tell you your position here. You have no position. We both know that the apartment you lived in with Jewelz was in his name. I had the spare key. While you were on your way here, his things were moved out by some people I trust. The spare key is on your dresser. I have a copy of his will. He gave specific instructions about his estate before he met you, and he updated it only to say that you can have the furniture and the lease was to be paid. So, you get furniture, and you get to live rent-free until the lease is up. His wife, who is the beneficiary of everything, has made the funeral arrangements with her sons and my parents. Now, we actually had a thought to make sure you had a place with the family, but since you like to show up and act like a donkey, you can find yourself sitting somewhere else. But keep in mind, if you even breathe hard, I will come and personally toss you out of the church door! Remember, I am my brother's keeper. Mesalyn has her own brothers, and I know you do not want that type of handling. Now, take this tissue since my dad's handkerchief has had it, get it together, and you can come in. We are not playing with you, so if you start some crap in this house, remember you are a good half mile from the front gate of this estate." Jasmyn got up and walked back to the home she grew up in. She smiled at her dad as if to say all is well.

Destiny, for all her shock, sat there for several minutes before getting it together and going to the family house. She smiled, and when asked who she was, she said she was a friend of Jewelz. Mesalyn tried to be nice and include Destiny in some of the fun and banter as the family and friends laughed at some of the memories Jewelz left them with. It was not long before Destiny left without saying goodbye.

When the paper came out the next day, the obituary section showed two obituaries for Jewelz! Sister Bernetha called me to see if I had seen it, and there it was: one obituary showing those left behind including Mesalyn, and the second one showing those left behind without Mesalyn but showing Destiny as his lifelong love!

Now, the funeral was very nice! Jewelz was looking like a sleeping man all dressed up in a designer suit! The makeup artist the funeral home uses is known to make you look great in death! I wonder about using him while I am living to make me look younger!

The casket was very nice and contained photos of angels on the inside so that when they closed the casket, should the dead open his eyes that is what he would see! There were so many flowers and pictures at the head and the foot of the casket showing all the many faces of Jewelz with his family. It was a beautiful church scene as everyone wore different vibrant colors to celebrate Jewelz's life. The immediate family wore different shades of blue and gray, the colors of Jewelz's favorite sports team. The program was also tastefully done showing Jewelz as a baby to adulthood, wedding pictures as well as pictures of him with his children at various ages. One thing I was very surprised to see was a picture at the end of the page with Destiny in it. I just knew the family would cut her completely out, but I was wrong. Sister Bernetha and I wondered if she was going to get her request to sit with the family.

The choir took their place, and the organist began to play softly as the viewing began. The request was that more upbeat hymns and gospel songs fill the church. His parents, while they were saddened by the passing of their son, wanted it to be a true celebration. Mesalyn agreed and provided suggestions to the Minister of Music so that the request was clear. People filed in to view the body and console the family. The twin girls were not there for the viewing, as Mesalyn felt that would be too much for the now four-year-olds. Mesalyn was beautiful, as always, smiling and greeting people as they came from the casket.

While the viewing all started very solemn and organized, I looked up, and there was Destiny, dressed in a designer black dress. I could tell it was designer because it was cut perfectly for her body. She had on a black hat and stiletto shoes with gold trim to match. Initially, no one paid her any attention only to notice she was the only one dressed in all black. But then, she did something crazy. After she went to the casket, stood crying, and spoke softly to Jewelz, she took a position at the front right pew. She never went to say anything to the family. Jasmyn looked over and whispered something to her mother and then her brother on the left side of her. A few moments after she stood there, several people came in, also in black, to view the body. That group one by one turned not to speak to the family but to speak to Destiny! After they gave her a grandiose hug and condolences, they sat down on the front right pew. Mesalyn gave them no attention and continued to greet those who came over with a smile and conversation.

It was clear what was going on! Destiny planned to have her own funeral at the same time!

Jasmyn was hot, and I could tell. That woman was my best pupil when I taught Sunday School! I loved her like she was my own! Partly because she was my goddaughter, but her spirit kept me laughing. She could have been my daughter for sure! I could read her almost as well as her parents. It was only a matter of time before one of those Mason children cleared that right front pew! Mesalyn had her own brothers, and I can tell you they were looking on making sure their sister was not bothered by what was taking place.

Well, as if that Destiny mess was not enough, there was this tall woman, dressed in red of all colors! The dress she had on was cut so that you did not need to wonder if she was wearing Spanx contraptions to hold you in. She didn't need it! She was in the shape I was in before I had my fifth baby! She had makeup on, but it was not waterproof, and I could tell that because there were streaks of makeup running down her cheeks. She, too, wore those stiletto shoes, and they were black with red trim. She just about fell into the casket crying over Jewelz! The funeral usher had to go over and pull her up! Mesalyn gave her in-laws a puzzled look and tried to keep her composure. At this point, Rev. Mason could see that if something was not done, very quietly, this viewing could turn into something else. Mrs. Mason whispered something to Rev. Mason, and he appeared relaxed. The lady in red stood on her own after a moment and turned to walk to the family when she glanced over and saw Destiny. She looked at her, and her eyes narrowed. She stood staring at Destiny for a moment, and just as she took the first step toward her, she stopped, laughed at her, and then turned to Mesalyn. She came over with her hand extended and shook Mesalyn's hand. She bowed her head and appeared to apologize to her for something. Mesalyn clearly accepted what the woman said, and they embraced each other. Well, would you believe she was one of the women that Jewelz had slept with? The lady in red went on to offer condolences to the family. Jasmyn knew who this woman was, and I suspect Mesalyn did as well. Both ladies are something!

More people filed in, most of them providing comfort to the family and wondering who the lady was standing opposite Mesalyn in the front pew. What a mess! I wish I could tell you that nothing else took place, but I can't do that. Do you know several more women came there to offer condolences and apologies to Mesalyn including her former friend Dion? I think I would have gone over and slapped Jewelz across his dead face and slammed the casket shut!

The viewing lasted an hour, and Destiny was still holding firm her position on that front right pew. At this point, the whispering reached everyone in the church as to who she was, and many of the seasoned folks were giving her long stares and disgusted looks.

Just before the funeral started, Mesalyn went for her twin girls. The plan was to have a final viewing just before the actual funeral, close the casket, and begin the service.

The minister officiating over the service was none other than the Right Reverend Doctor Donald P. Kingston. In all my life, this man was by far one of the best at presiding over a funeral! He could make the devil repent after one of his funeral sermons! Dr. Kingston was informed of the delicate situation that developed during the viewing. He was able to observe that Destiny was in the right front pew, and the family was in the left front pew. He was clearly not pleased. He stood up and asked those who have not had time to view the body to please come. At that moment, the ushers stood next to Destiny, who at this point was puzzled.

The usher whispered to her that she should go to the casket to say her final goodbye. Mistakenly, Destiny thought she was going be the last to see Jewelz, and she gave a slight grin as if she won. She went up, with the usher, said some words to Jewelz, and was reaching up to close the casket when the usher very calmly brought her hands down. In whispers, the usher told her the funeral home will do that, and she took her back to her seat.

Seeing that no one else needed to come to the casket, with a gentle nod of his head, a group of men came up, surrounded the casket, and with arms interlocked, said some words to their friend, Jewelz. This was a fraternity-like group of men who came to support the family and honor their dead brother. After they were finished, like armed guards, they widened their tight circle to let just the family in. Destiny was more puzzled than ever! She wanted to stand up, but the usher had her hand on her shoulder serving a double purpose: to comfort and if need be and to restrain! I forgot to tell y'all the usher was Sister Bernetha!

The men blocked the view of most of the congregation, except those on the balcony. One by one, starting with Jewelz's siblings, his parents, children, and finally Mesalyn, the family said their goodbyes. Jewelz's sons closed the casket with the director of the funeral home guiding them. When they were done, the men opened the circle, and the family took their seats.

The rest of the funeral went on with Dr. Kingston

preaching as if his life depended on it! Several people were moved to joyful tears as they stood to clap, and others remained seated excited about what Dr. Kingston was preaching. When the funeral ended, the processional order was the casket leading the exit, the immediate family, and finally everyone else but in the order the ushers directed. Well, as one final act in the church, Destiny attempted to go around Sister Bernetha. When she made her move, Sister Bernetha gave her a sharp look just as two ushers came up to remind Destiny that this was not the place for foolishness. All this was happening under the watchful eye of Jasmyn. I believe that woman would beat the days and nights out of Destiny had it not been that we were in church!

At the graveside, we got the flowers arranged around the grave, and the casket was in place. Rev. Kingston gave the burial sermon, and someone began singing in the distance. It was all beautiful and done so tastefully! Destiny got to the cemetery late and was distraught. She sat in the car crying as people walked by looking and wondering why she was even there. All the mistresses that showed up made sure to keep their distance at this point, but clearly, all of them had an issue with Destiny. One even knocked on her car window. When Destiny opened it a little to hear what the lady in red wanted, the lady in red hissed, "You were not the only one!" Destiny put the window up and cried even more!

No one saw Destiny again that day. Jasmyn was ready

to remind her of her place, but it appears Destiny got the message. Sister Bernetha said that Destiny really thought that she should have gotten better treatment from the family. She clearly did not know whom she was talking to, as Sister Bernetha let her know that she was lucky she did not catch a whooping for coming and for the position she took by sitting in the right front pew. According to Sister Bernetha, Destiny was shaken having clearly realized she made a mistake. She had asked her friends to come for support, and they came through for her not knowing the entire problem that it presented. A couple of those friends heard what Sister Bernetha said and were immediately upset that they were involved in the mess.

4

Tidewater Family Funeral and Black History Month Sunday Dinner

Here we are, the last Sunday in February, closing our Black History Month celebrations. You should have seen that sea of Kente cloth and other bright colors we all wore. The pastor said that on only one Sunday should we wear all black, and that was the Sunday the church published information in a program about those who were slain before and during the Civil Rights movement. They were careful to choose only those people slain most of us never heard about. Like whole towns that were slain! Like the Black Wall Street in Oklahoma, and the Rosewood Massacre! I heard of these types of things happening, but to read the details was something!

I won't bore you with the details of our shopping trip. It

was the usual except now our driver was to be Joanna from now on. I made sure that I went to the restroom before we got in Joe's truck! She wanted to help, and we all agreed that it was nice of her. Besides, we have to train the young folk to take over some time.

One thing I could never understand is how folks my age are not willing to let the next generation of worshippers take over! When will we get our rest if we keep them from learning from us?

Before we left for the food warehouse, we always go over the menu, check the pantry to see what we need, and check the calendar to make sure that other functions had what they needed, and then, we take off to the food warehouse. After we finished that, Sister Bernetha and I went out to the car to meet Joanna and Joe.

As Joanna was pulling off, we saw Sister Tidewater walking toward the truck dressed in a hot red sweat suit, with red tennis shoes waving her hands as if something was wrong. Sister Bernetha muttered, "Run her over." I jokingly pushed her arm as we both chuckled.

Joanna slowed to a stop and opened her window as Joe leaned over to hear what was going on.

"Hello, Sister Tidewater! Is everything alright?" Joe asked

"Good morning! Everything is just fine! Hello, Joanna, Sister Vista, Sister Bernetha," Sister Tidewater said with a quick wave. "I just wanted to make sure you did not forget that there is a funeral taking place the Thursday before the Black History Month closing Sunday Dinner. That funeral is for one of my beloved relatives, and we know good food, and we love to eat lots of it. The family is using this church as I suggested because we require more space than the home church of the deceased. I saw that you were leaving and assumed that you were headed to the food warehouse. I want to make sure y'all don't short us on any food at the repast. Now, the menu for the repast has been prepared, and I don't want anything left out for the repast. I wondered if I could come along to make sure all is taken care of, but I see there is really not enough room between Sister Bernetha and Sister Vista! Y'all know y'all got some hips, now!" Sister Tidewater chuckled as if it was a joke. Sister Bernetha opened the door to the truck, and I grabbed her hand before she could lift her leg to get out. She slammed the door closed just as fast as she opened it and looked at me as if to say I saved a life!

"Calm down, girl. She isn't getting in this truck. She just wants to agitate somebody," I said very quietly.

Joe spoke up having seen from the corner of his eye that Sister Bernetha was about to have a little talk with Sister Tidewater. "Well, Sister Tidewater, we are pretty good at doing this job. We have been doing it for years now. Joanna is learning her part, and right now, she is driving us up to the food warehouse. We have indeed considered everything that we need for the funeral as well as other programs taking place this upcoming week. We have the menu, and Sisters Vista and Bernetha are great at making sure there were extra plates because we know that some people want to take food home. We always season the food just right, and people have even asked us to consider starting a catering business. But we declined because we are satisfied with the service. Unless something was forgotten on the menu, we ..."

"Oh, Joe!" Sister Tidewater interrupted. "I tell you what. My family is very organized and thorough. Everything you see on that menu is what we will be looking forward to on Thursday after we funeralize our beloved. It sounds like you all have it all under control, so I will go about my regular duties for the day. I am working out and trying to keep in shape. You know Sister Bernetha and Sister Vista, it looks like you could stand to come and work out with me! One of these days, we will get a little older, and we want to hold on to these bodies. We don't want to show up in heaven looking too flabby, now do we? Well, have a good trip, and if you need anything, I hope you will come back or give me a call. Joanna, you are doing a good job! You have everyone buckled in and ready to go! Keep up the great work. You are so beautiful!" Sister Tidewater then turned and walked back to her car.

Joanna put the window up, and we all just sat there for a moment. Joanna was the first to speak up. "Daddy, there is something wrong with that woman," Joanna said with a concerned tone.

"Joanna, everybody has some sort of spiritual problem. That is why we as the body of Christ have to try to do better. We get to see these people and learn from them and help them when we are supposed to. What you will learn here, little girl, is that not everybody who says they are a Christian is a Christian. Some people do good, but they are a little messy, and they need to be cleaned up. The church is a hospital. Remember that. Now, let's get on over to the food warehouse."

As we were making our way back to the church, we discussed how the menu for the funeral was different from the usual. The question then came up about who was paying the bill. Was it the church like we do for members or was the family being billed or paid in advance? Sister Bernetha was on the trustee board and the finance board, so it was something she would look into if for no other reason than to make sure all was done properly, and no one was taking advantage of the church.

In the past, people would do their best to take advantage of the church by way of membership. The stories I could tell! I remember this one family, the Greens joined the church for the sole purpose of taking advantage of the benefit of a repast for a dying relative. Can you believe that!? But I tell you one thing, they were able to have that repast in our church, free and all because they were members. We didn't see them again until another family member passed. Well, they were surprised when they came to meet with the

Bereavement Committee and were told that they rescinded their membership via letter just after the last funeral. The very family member who passed sent the letter saying that they were moving on to another church, but they thanked our church for all they did to make their time there a pleasant one! Now, the dead and the family thought there would be no cost for the repast! The best that the committee could do was to allow them the use of the church, but the food would have to be brought in or the family could pay the cost of the food the church provided. Well, shocked or not, they held that funeral here; the food was all provided by the family except the meat. The family paid the church for the meat because as one family member put it, they did not want to entrust that to anyone in the family!

When we had all the food labeled and put away, we sat down to make sure we had enough hands to prep and cook for the upcoming event—the Tidewater Funeral. We had all the supplies we needed, and I suggested we label and put aside anything we were using for that function. This way, we could just jump in and work when the time came.

It was Thursday, I and the usual crew had several members who work solely to assist in the funeral repast. The service window was open as people came by to drop off desserts and other items that were to be served during the repast. The room was decorated very nicely with the deceased favorite colors. Tables for the dessert were set up with several vases of fresh flowers—also a request of the family.

Sister Bernetha reported that anything that seemed above and beyond our usual was actually paid for by the family. The fresh flowers were an example. We usually use silk arrangements, but the family said the deceased had very specific instructions, and they wanted to make sure to follow them to the letter. The deceased was the cousin to Sister Tidewater; her name was Cindi. Apparently, they were very close, and she wanted to be sure that everything was done as her Cindi wanted. The Bereavement Ministry saw no reason not to allow that since the family was actually reasonable regarding the cost and what could be done.

As the viewing started upstairs, we were all working to make sure the cooked food stayed warm, like the greens, green beans, and cabbage. The meats were all cooking, and the timing was going to be tight, but we have never served late, so we were not worried. The meats included chicken, turkey wings, and beef. There were also stuffed filets of soles as well as a vegetable medley. There were candied yams, Mac n cheese, stuffing with gravy, white, and brown rice. There were homemade rolls from a family member who clearly knew how to use the yeast! Those rolls were golden brown and pretty! There was a fruit salad, a cheese platter with crackers, and a vegetable platter complete with several types of dips. At the request of the family, the green salad was to have no sign of any iceberg lettuce in it. I like that option too as it is supposed to be better for you. Overall, the requests were not too bad, especially with Sister Tidewater being involved!

The dessert table had a center cake that had a picture of the deceased on it. Apparently, the bakery sent it to express their condolences. She was a frequent customer of the bakery, and they wanted to do something for the family. The cake was raspberry-filled, and the raspberries were fresh! The other desserts came from the organizations that Cindi was involved in. They wanted to do something, and Sister Tidewater did not trust anyone she did not know personally providing any other dish besides dessert. They each brought in desserts, and some commented that they brought items that they loved and knew that Cindi would enjoy. It was truly beautiful to see the outpouring from so many people. Cindi was clearly going to be missed. She was loved too, poor thing.

The room was festive for a repast. The family requested that some type of Gospel Jazz music play during the repast. There were family members who checked in early before the start of the funeral to say that they would be there to help serve after the funeral. I told them to come, and we made sure they ate first, since they were family, and especially when you start serving; before you know it, the food you want is gone! The family brought in a case of those folding take-out containers so that people can take food home. The other request, left up to the family who volunteered to serve, was to make sure that there were take-out containers for several family members who could not be there. Sister Bernetha made a note to be sure that as soon as the meat was finished, she would make sure they got it.

The family was just returning from the Gate of Heaven Cemetery when Sister Tidewater rushed in. She was moving fast as she pulled off her fascinator and her suit jacket at the same time!

"Alright, I am here! What needs to be done!? What does not taste right!? What needs to be sampled?" She yelled as if she oversaw the event!

"Ellie, what are you shouting about? These folks took care of everything including the food for Uncle Tibbi and Aunt Shane. We are covered here, so you can go find a seat and wait for the rest of the family. Calm your nerves! Cindi said I should make sure you did nothing more after helping her make her own arrangements. Now, go find a seat, and I promise I will come to get you if we need anything," Millicent, Sister Tidewater's cousin and Cindi's sister said.

"Ok. Ok, you're right. I did a lot, and I do need to sit down somewhere. This has been a long day for me. I know it has been for you too, cousin. Thank you for giving me a break. Are you sure though? This was your—"

"Yes, I am sure! I enjoy helping like this. I am fine. Now, please go sit down."

"I am gone." Sister Tidewater put her suit jacket back on and sat down with a sigh of relief.

Just then, Millicent turned to me and smirked, "I don't

know how y'all deal with her. She is my family, but if there was a trade like they do in professional sports, she would be the first I would get rid of!"

Just like that, Sister Bernetha and I fell into a belly laugh, so strong I found myself wondering if I pulled something in my gut!

Everything went well, and we received compliments from Cindi's boyfriend and other family members that they were pleased with our service. Sister Tidewater wanted to disagree with some things, but each of her family would draw her in to say "Yes, everything was great." They knew how messy she was!

Now, we had to make sure to turn that kitchen around so that on Friday morning, that prep team could get in there and start things for our Sunday Black History closing dinner. We had that kitchen sparkling like we were never there earlier serving that big dinner!

Thankfully, I was not due back in that kitchen until Saturday. I needed to make sure that what was needed in preparation was prepared and that anything that needed chopping, cleaning, or anything last minute could be done. We always had one thing that may be missed by the Friday folk, and that was ok. We do a lot, and it is gonna happen, so none of us fuss over it. Now, if we were to get to Sunday, and someone forgot to get the meat, that would be a big problem!

Sunday came, and all the food was done, and we were

sitting pretty! I even had a chance to make those yeast rolls, with Sister Bernetha's help for the pastor's table. Next year, we said we would do enough for the main table. Seeing those rolls at the repast on Thursday inspired me!

As the people came in to eat dinner, I noticed that there were some new but familiar faces among the crowd. It dawned on me that it was some of the people from Cindi's funeral. I suspected that they were worshipping with Sister Tidewater before going their way. The nicest folk you ever want to meet!

The pastor already blessed the food just before the benediction in the sanctuary. But he stood up to comment before we began serving.

"Let me have everyone's attention for just a moment. Now, most of you know me. I shoot from the hip, as they say!" Everyone chuckled, knowing he was someone who told it like it was.

"Yes, but I try not to hurt but help. I see a few people here in the room that were not in service this morning. Now, I won't call you out because as I said before, I don't want to hurt! I said a blessing over this good food upstairs, and y'all missed it! So, because I want to help, y'all see how I did that. I am gonna repeat the blessing so that we all hear it! Is that alright?"

"Yes sir. Go ahead and bless the food," one person shouted

"Two blessings are better than one anytime, Preacher,"

someone else shouted.

With that, the pastor blessed the food, and we began serving. Everything was in order until that Sister Tidewater started doing what she does.

She marched into the kitchen as I was getting more food for the serving table and asked if I knew anything about those dinner rolls on the pastor's table. I told her I did since I was the one who made them. She appeared shocked and said, "You made them? Those rolls look like the rolls from Thursday's repast. Are you sure you made those rolls? They look like yeast rolls to me! If those are the rolls from the repast, someone is ..."

I put my hand up and turned my head just as Sister Bernetha was walking in.

"Sister Tidewater, today is not the day for this kind of foolishness. Now as I said, I made those rolls. I did not have time, even with Sister Bernetha's help to make enough for the serving table. We were able to give away all the food from your family's repast, and there was nothing left over. Now, I have things to do, and unless you want to help, please leave this kitchen and enjoy your dinner." I acted like she was gone and went on with what I was in the kitchen for.

Sister Bernetha stood there staring at Sister Tidewater and finally said, "Sister Vista made those rolls, and I helped her. I hope you don't think this Ministry would do what you are accusing us of doing?"

Sister Tidewater walked out of the kitchen embarrassed

but not so much that she did not head straight for the pastor's table and ask for a roll, claiming she needed to swallow a pill. They gave her what she asked for, and when she tasted the roll, only then did she appear to be satisfied.

5

Ms. Christianne Lanae' Bevington

Every church will suffer through various scandals, and our church is no different. I have to tell you about the other mess that happened here some other time.

Every Sunday, the minister that is preaching will come forth after the preached word to ask if anyone wants to join the church. It is not different in most churches; the minister comes down from the pulpit to make the plea as the choir sings in the background. When someone goes to the altar, the congregation claps and praises God for a soul saved.

There are four ways that a person becomes a member: restoring membership after being away for a long time; joining the church for the first time; joining the church and wanting to be baptized; and finally, joining under watch care. Watchcare is usually for the young person who is too young to say they are joining, but the parents want to make sure that they are linked or members of the church.

This one Sunday, Rev. Nelson, one of our assistant ministers, preached a great word, and the church was on fire! Folks were waving the flag of surrender all over the sanctuary, i.e. they had their hands raised to heaven. I was caught up too! That man can truly preach! When he opened the doors for people to join the church, three people went up to become members. One woman, whose name I did not catch, was particularly anxious, so much so that she practically ran up to Rev. Nelson and hugged him. The hug caught him off guard so much so that he stumbled. She had a good grip on him, so he did not fall.

She was an attractive young woman, at least younger than Rev. Nelson. After she provided her information to the deacons, the church clapped as the new members were introduced to the church. The three people, including the young woman, went to receive the information about being a member and when they would receive the Right Hand of Fellowship, making them official members.

Later, I learned that the young lady's name was Christianne. She had two children but never brought them to church. I figured maybe they were too young or something like that. She would sit on the balcony except for Sundays when Rev. Nelson was preaching. On those Sundays, she would sit in the front pew, and her dress would always find itself rising above her knees! The usher would always have to grab something to help her stay covered, but she would always "drop" the cover when Rev. Nelson approached the podium to preach. You could tell he noticed what message she was sending because he would break out into a sweat and never look to the left side of the church the whole time he preached!

Well, since she was not getting Rev. Nelson's attention that way, she would be sure to greet him after services. The ushers and ministerial staff noticed she would not shake the hands of anyone else except Rev. Nelson. He was very uncomfortable, and though he hid it, it was clear that he might have been a little scared! He was a strong man, but I imagine that he was thinking about what he may have done to have someone obsess over him. Christianne was indeed obsessed.

One weekday, Christianne called in to say she needed spiritual counseling but would only speak to Rev. Nelson. When Shelly, the secretary for the assistant ministers, took down her information and relayed it to Rev. Nelson, he was ok, and he should be ok. After all, she needed something that maybe he could help her with.

Shelly called Christianne, nicknamed Chrissy, to come in and gave her an appointment date. When Chrissy showed up at the church, she was dressed in one of those body-clenching dresses. Not being the one to judge since we don't know what is going on, the deaconess assigned to be in the room during the meeting was well-reserved but observing. Deaconess Lynnie Mathers is not one to cross when it comes to doing things the right way. She was the one deaconess that the ministers called when they would be meeting with members for various reasons. Lynnie greeted Chrissy and told her to have a seat while they wait for Rev. Nelson to finish with another member.

When the office door opened, Chrissy stood up so fast that she nearly stumbled! Lynnie went over to Rev. Nelson to say that they were ready to come in as soon as he was. Chrissy spoke up then.

"Excuse me. I have a meeting at this time with Rev. Nelson. I prefer to speak to him in private. We are both adults, and I am sure that he can handle what my needs are."

Deaconess Lynnie, smiling sweetly, said, "Oh, yes. You do have an appointment; however, our rules are simple here to protect the members and clergy. There is always a female deaconess with the minister when counseling the opposite sex. Now, if you feel there is something you need to say that is so personal, arrangements can be made."

"Please make arrangements," Chrissy said. "What I need to say I want only Rev. Nelson to hear."

At that moment, Chrissy was staring at Rev. Nelson as if she was hungry and he was food! Lynnie saw it too and was right on top of what needed to take place next.

"Come with me, young lady. I will show you to the counseling suite." Lynnie began to walk down the hall with Chrissy following close behind like she was in a hurry.

The counseling suite was a small section of the church

with two offices and two counseling rooms. The rooms and offices shared a wall that had a glass window. You may have seen the windows in daycare places. The room is soundproof so that you can have a private session, but someone could see what was going on. I have to tell you about that time that window came in handy!

When Lynnie showed Chrissy in, she stepped back out so that Rev. Nelson could take his place in the room across from Chrissy. Lynnie sat outside on the other side of the glass window. She could not hear what was being said.

According to Lynnie, she could see the smile drain from Rev. Nelson as Chrissy began to talk and her dress rise above her knee. The dress stopped just above her knee, but her knees were not kept together for long! A couple of times, she licked her finger while talking to Rev. Nelson, and he moved back when she tried to touch him. At one point, Lynnie knew she needed to interrupt the session when Chrissy seemed to keep moving closer to Rev. Nelson.

She opened the door and said, "Is it ok in here?"

Rev. Nelson said firmly, "Deaconess Lynnie, we are all done. In the future, Ms. Chrissy will be meeting with someone else on the ministerial staff for her spiritual needs. Please help her to the exit as we are finished here. Ms. Chrissy, thank you for speaking candidly to me today. I hope you will take the advice I gave you. I am asking that you do not reach out to me in the future until you can get the professional help you need."

"I need you, Rev. Nelson. I am sure of it. While it may not be what you see now, I am sure that you need me too. I am not ashamed of what I feel, and I will shout it from the top of this building to anyone who will listen. I think you should give us a try."

"Hold on, young lady," Lynnie said. "This is not appropriate at all. If you have some type of spiritual need, the clergy here are willing to help you. Flirting with this minister is not appropriate, and this is hardly the place for that. Let me show you out."

Lynnie stood in front of Rev. Nelson and pointed to the door. As Chrissy walked out, she said over her shoulder, "You will see me at church on Sunday, Rev. Nelson." Lynnie looked at Rev. Nelson as if to reassure him that she too would be in church to have his back.

Sunday morning came, and there was no sign of Chrissy. Just after the service started and the ushers opened the doors for people to be seated, there was Chrissy. The usher on the aisle was directing her to an empty seat, but she kept moving right past her. Chrissy had on a low-cut short dress that was loose fitting enough that if she bent forward or bent over, you were sure to know what color her underwear was … if she had any on!

Chrissy sat on the front pew toward the center, just within eyesight of Rev. Nelson, who had not seen her come in. When she sat down, the dress sat mid-thigh, and she did not keep her knees together! Clearly, she fully intended for Rev. Nelson to see something under that dress, but he missed it because Rev. Kate saw her first and began coughing! Poor Rev. Kate grabbed her extra shawl and began moving toward Chrissy. Rev. Nelson looking puzzled was watching where Rev. Kat was going, and the usher met Rev. Kate at the edge of the pulpit to see what was wrong. When she told the usher and pointed, the usher gasp loudly and moved quickly to cover Chrissy up! Before the usher could get to Chrissy, Rev. Nelson looked in the direction that Rev. Kate had pointed, and he too gasped loudly! He quickly looked away, embarrassed by what he saw. Chrissy had decided not to wear panties with that dress and clearly wanted Rev. Nelson to know she wanted something more than spiritual direction from him! The scandal that day in the church! Rev. Kate went and sat right down next to that nasty Chrissy and whispered in her ear just after she was covered by the usher. First Lady Worthy came over thinking there was a medical issue only to learn what the commotion was! She was not happy, and she sat on the opposite side of Chrissy and whispered in the other ear. When she went to remove the shawl from her lap, First Lady whispered something else in her ear that caused the young woman to freeze in place. She moved to fold her hands on her lap, and her face went from a look of defiance to defeat. Rev. Kate took her place back in the pulpit and leaned in to reassure Rev. Nelson that the situation was being handled.

Just then, Sister Bernetha came over and sat down next

to Chrissy. Chrissy looked at Sister Bernetha who looked as if to say "don't try it!"

Rev. Nelson preached a sermon that almost seemed to be directly for Chrissy. It was about loose women and men! He talked about Jezebel and all her foolishness and how her behavior then is no different from some of these women out there today. He even made it clear that any man that would take up time with a woman who has no morals, no faith in God through Jesus, and no respect for herself is in big trouble. When Rev. Nelson called those who wanted prayer to the altar, Chrissy whispered to the First Lady, and together, they went to the altar to pray. Sister Bernetha joined them holding the young woman's hand. Chrissy began to cry, and at one point, she put her head on the shoulder of the First Lady. When the prayer ended, Chrissy hurried out of the church. I guess she realized she had done something crazy. What woman shows a man her business in church while he is sitting in the pulpit too?

Several people in the congregation thought Chrissy was sick, and that is why she needed attention. No one who knew or saw what happened spoke of it. It was too unbelievable. The church takes in people who are "sick," but no one could prepare for that kind of sick or boldness.

6

Little Miss Lyndsy

There was a couple in our congregation that at the age of 65 found themselves fostering a little girl named Lyndsy T. I don't want to give out her last name since the family prefers it that way until all the legal stuff is finalized.

Now, the couple, Jeff and Nina, had two adult children who were on their own and thriving in great careers. Jeff and Nina were enjoying their grandchildren and all the joys of being grandparents. One day, Nina was reading an article about the foster care system and how it was broken. The article had interviews with caseworkers, foster parents, and even some young adults who grew up in foster care. The article moved Nina to talk to Jeff about being a foster parent. He agreed, having known people who were foster parents when their children were growing up. He had one rule, no teenagers. I am sure we understood why.

They went through the process, and up until they met Lyndsy, most of the foster children were able to be reunited with their families. Others were adopted after failed attempts to reunite them with their family.

But then came little Miss Lyndsy, with her cute self. I saw that little girl, and I knew she was an angel! Yes, some children are born into bad situations, and that was the case for this child.

Her parents were married, divorced just before she was born, and fought about everything. What landed 8-year-old Lyndsy in foster care was both her parents were involved with drugs and drinking. They both were fighting to keep Lyndsy safe until the drugs set in. Now, for two people to be divorced, you would think they would just move on with their lives, but not these two crazy people! If he was dating, Mom would fight! If Mom was dating, the father would lose it!

Whenever Lyndsy was with her mom, her mom stayed sober. The same when she was with her father. But after a while, the mom would tell her ex to come to get Lyndsy earlier than they had arranged, and he initially thought he would use that to get custody. But then his demons started weighing on him just like his ex-wife and having Lyndsy early was interfering with a "schedule" of drug and alcohol abuse he set for himself. Lyndsy's mom had a "schedule" too and that was why she wanted Lyndsy at her dad's early.

Well, that created a fight until the day her dad left poor

Lyndsy on the front steps of the apartment building by herself in the cold winter! According to him, he dropped her off at the time he was supposed to, and it is not his fault; the mom was not there to get her! The mom came home, and on a drug/alcohol high, she did not even realize the time and just went on about her business ... straight to bed! Now, I can only think that she was already home high and drunk when she walked into the building and missed seeing her child at the door. It took the social workers two days before they reached either one of those parents! By that time, someone had already found Lyndsy and brought her to the police station as a lost child. That night, she was in her first emergency placement foster home!

Cutting the long story short, neither parent could get it together to get that poor child back. The family did not want to deal with the parents and felt she was better off with a new family. Can you believe that? The grandparents did request to still be in the picture if the adopted family would allow it. They were up in age and did not want Lyndsy not to know her people.

Jeff and Nina were all too ready to take that little girl into their home! Their family thought it was a great idea after meeting Lyndsy that she should stay because she seemed to fit right in!

After the home visits, counseling, meetings with social workers, and doctors' appointments, finally, the time came for the adoption to be made final! Jeff and Nina announced that they were having a baby, and we all thought that was too funny! Pastor and First Lady went to the courthouse to be witnesses. Just like that, she was their daughter and a part of our church family!!

I tell you, that little girl was so happy to have Jeff and Nina in her life! She is involved in the youth choir; she plays the piano; she does gymnastics and has expressed a desire to even play soccer, just as her new older sister did! I love a happy ending, and Lord knows that was an ending these children today need!

Now, I shared this story about Jeff and Nina because we all need to know that we need to help people the way the Lord leads us. Had Nina not been a big reader of everything, they might not have ever become foster parents and met Little Miss Lyndsy T!

7

Rev. Dr. Ben Jonathan Worthy

It was just after one of the best-preached words I have ever heard from Pastor Worthy that we got word he fell ill. We were all headed home when the call came in that he had to be rushed to the hospital from his house. I was never so glad those children of mine got me to start using a cell phone! I was in the Pastor's Aid Ministry for some time, and they called me because First Lady would surely be looking for me. I got home, changed clothes, and headed back out to the hospital.

When I got there, the chair of deacons, Deacon Booker, was there. He was sitting with several people who are currently in the Pastor's Aid Ministry. There were several deaconesses there, and the chair of the Trustee Ministry. I asked where the assistant pastor was, and Deacon Booker told me she was en route. Just then, Rev. Kanklon rushed in.

"Good afternoon, Deacon Booker. Everyone! Do we have any updates? Where is First Lady?"

"Rev. K, we do not have any updates at this point. First Lady is in the back with the pastor right now. They are allowing her to stay with him until they move him upstairs to ICU. They believe he had a stroke, but the tests are pending. We just need to keep on praying. He is not conscious. But they were able to stabilize him here. We are thankful that First Lady saw the signs and got him help!"

"Thank God! I will see if I can get back there to say a word of prayer," Rev. Kanklon was visibly shaken at the thought that his friend might have had a stroke. He went to the registration desk, and they buzzed him in to see the pastor.

Deacon Booker came over and pulled me to the side.

"Vista, you and I have seen a lot over the years. This is going to be a tough one. If the pastor is in bad shape, we need to pull in some ministers to cover the church while he recovers. Pastor Worthy is one of the best, and certainly, at such a young age, I don't want to lose him. If he decides to retire, my Lord, remember when we first came here and how crazy it was when we had to get a new pastor?"

"Yes, I sure do remember! I thought I was going to run away from that building and never come back!" I remember it like it was yesterday. Power struggles, accusations of cheating, accusations of blasphemy, and accusations of all kinds from people who wanted one minister against everyone who wanted a different minister!

"We just need to keep on praying. Strokes today do not mean the end of life, thank God! If you get them help early, people who have a stroke really can survive and recover with no residual issues. My prayer is that it will be what is going to happen to our Pastor Worthy. He is young and in great shape, thanks to that new thing. What is Orange Therapy? Orange Thought?"

"You mean Orange Fury!" Deacon Booker and I laughed. I love to walk, and a long time ago I was what they called a runner, but as time went on, I knew I better slow down. I am not in bad shape, but I don't like to run so much anymore.

"Let's just hold fast for now until we can get some answers. The deacons have a meeting scheduled for next Saturday, so thankfully there is time to really get what we need so that we can put a plan together. Vista, I am going to look to you for support and prayer. Sister, we are gonna make it!"

"Yes, we most certainly will make it! So will Pastor Worthy! Now, let's huddle over here with the others and start praying." Just then, the assistant pastor rushed in.

"Deacon Booker! My God, how is Pastor Worthy? Lord, have mercy. I have rushed here praying the entire way! This is ..."

"Calm down. We are just waiting for the update. Rev. K. is back there now. Let's see if we can get them to let you in. The Worthy children should be here any minute." Deacon

Booker walked the assistant pastor to the registration desk. The door buzzed, and they let her go in.

After an hour, we were notified that they moved Pastor Worthy to the ICU, still unconscious but stable. First Lady Worthy came out to tell us that he was in God's hands and that we should all go home and continue to lift the family in prayer. The Worthy children were at their father's side.

Before we left, we all gathered in a circle for prayer, and people whom we did not know joined us! We prayed for their loved ones as well. God does that sometimes ... you know bringing strangers together to pray. I love it! As we all left the hospital, I couldn't help but feel a tinge, just a slight tinge of worry that our beloved pastor might be in trouble.

8

Shirley Benita Harris

In my lifetime, I have had very few regrets. I was always taught to think first before making any decisions about my life or my family. Sometimes though, I think that you have to just decide and think later! It is not something we should do all the time, but if your gut and heart say go ahead, well, go ahead!

Back when our youngest child was sixteen or seventeen years old, my dear husband and I were just as tickled to be getting the house to ourselves! You know, no children around, something like a quiet time until they come to visit. All our children were raised well. Yes, I say so myself! With our baby now preparing for life, we were just glowing parents guiding the last young mind.

For years, I knew the Harris family. Some of their children grew up with my children. One child in particular,

Shirley, took a liking to me. I guess I saw her as one of my favorites because y'all know, I love children! Especially, the babies! Oh, I can hold a baby all day—two babies if they are available! Just to see their little faces and watch them figure out the world has always been something I enjoyed.

Now, Shirley was raised right. Her parents were just like us and wanted nothing more than to have our children succeed in life. We don't mean like doctors and lawyers, but successful, like, being able to take care of themselves.

Shirley lost her way after high school. She took up with the one wrong person, a man, and he gave her something that she could not live without—heroin. When she was on that stuff, she was a mess! She would disappear for long periods, come back to her parent's house, and beg for forgiveness and help. She even robbed them while they watched her! She was so crazy! All Mr. and Mrs. Harris could do was pray and prepare for the next thing she would try to do to raise the money for the heroin.

Then one day, Shirley came home upset. I was there when she came through the front door hollering for her mom. Ms. Harris almost fell over as she yelled so loud.

Shirley said she thought she might be pregnant. By that time, she was around twenty-two or twenty-three years old. Her face was still so beautiful! But you could not trust her at all. You had to be very careful. When she saw me, she was embarrassed, but I gave her a look that said I still loved her.

Mrs. Harris and I sat her down, and after lemonade and

a sandwich, Shirley started her story. She said if she was pregnant, she would stop doing drugs and work to get clean. She asked if she could move back in with her parents. Her mother was very hesitant and told Shirley that she would need to speak to her dad. In the meantime, Shirley should work to show she means it this time to get clean. I believe if I was not there, Shirley would have exploded. I saw the way she inhaled deeply and looked at her mother as if she was being unreasonable. The look could cut rocks!

Shirley agreed to the terms and said she would come back that night to see her dad. Mrs. Harris gathered her things and asked me to come along with them to the clinic to confirm the pregnancy. I told them I would drive so that Mrs. Harris could take a break. This was a lot on her.

Well, when that nurse told Shirley she was certainly pregnant, I thought Mrs. Harris would faint. A pregnancy, a grandchild, and the mother on drugs. This was too much. When Mrs. Harris asked Shirley about the father, Shirley said it could be anyone! She was out there having sex with any man who could give her a hit!

Mr. Harris, given all the information, allowed Shirley to move back in. She was to attend a ninety-day program for heroin addicts. She was to make sure that she was taking care of her body so that the growing baby would stand a chance of survival, and be free of health problems.

To our surprise, Shirley did exactly what her parents asked of her! I was praying that the Lord would fix Shirley!

She would stop by whenever I had baked pie or cookies. She said the baby loved it! I loved it too! Shirley was back to the young lady I remembered ... if only that would last.

Shirley had a little girl and named her "Angel," saying that if it was not for her, she would still be on drugs or dead. The Harris family was so happy that all went well and Angel was healthy and such a bright-eyed baby. Shirley's siblings showed up for her when she went into labor, and they were there when little Angel was born. It was beautiful!

When little Angel turned 6 months old, Shirley came over to my house saying she heard I was baking. When I told her to come in, but I had not baked anything, she seemed disappointed. That did not give me a clue that anything was wrong. We enjoyed a light lunch, and she let me feed and cuddle little Angel. Shirley asked me to keep Angel while she ran to the store for more lemons to make lemonade. I thought that was odd since I did not need lemonade. But again, I got to thinking maybe she loved my lemonade and wanted me to make it. She was gone for thirty minutes, the time it takes to get there and back. When she did not have lemons, I asked what happened. She said they did not look good. I believed her.

She took Angel and went home.

I did not see Shirley for a week or so. When I went by the Harris' house, Mrs. Harris looked upset. She told me that Shirley was using that heroin again. Social Services came to the house to inquire about Angel. Apparently, one of the drug dealers called them to report a woman was carrying a baby while using in one of the drug houses. I am so glad they called, but a drug dealer with a conscience! Clearly, the angels were watching over little Angel!

Mr. Harris was out looking for Shirley, furious that she had thrown away an opportunity to get sober and stay sober! When he finally located her, she was in one of the drug houses, high, with little Angel sleeping in her baby stroller. The filth and stench were enough to make you sick! He did not bother to wake Shirley; he was so angry. He took a picture of her and Angel in that mess, took the stroller with Angel in it, and went home. When he got there, he threw the stroller away; Mrs. Harris changed and bathed Angel. The clothes and blankets she was wearing were tossed into a bag so that they too could be thrown away. Mr. Harris said he could still smell the stench from that drug house in those clothes!

Shirley came home the next day in a panic, the police in tow. She was hysterical telling her parents how she was out all night looking for little Angel after someone kidnapped her while she was sleeping at a friend's house. The Harris' knew that was a lie. The officer showed sympathy to Shirley trying to calm her down. When Mr. and Mrs. Harris did not show they were alarmed, the second officer asked if they knew anything about the missing baby. Mr. Harris, without a word, pulled out his cell phone and showed the officer the picture and the date and time he took the picture. The second officer appeared to be angry, but it was not clear who she was mad at. She got her male partner's attention, and after he sat Shirley down, he looked at the picture. They asked Mr. Harris to show them where the child was, and Mrs. Harris took them to Angel, who was safe in her room asleep.

Shirley was so distracted with her need to find her baby and possibly her need to get a fix, that she did not understand her baby was right there in the house. The officers came back to the front room where Shirley was to tell her that the baby was safe at home and that her father had actually taken the baby. Mr. Harris held up the picture from the night before, and immediately, Shirley flew into a rage. I was coming up the front steps to catch her lunging at her father! It was a full-on wrestling match with Mrs. Harris pulling Mr. Harris out of Shirley's reach, and the police grabbing Shirley to keep her from hitting her father!

While this was happening, I heard little Angel crying, and I announced I was going to take care of the baby. No one heard me, I guess.

Mr. Harris was still not saying a word. Shirley did all the talking:

"Officer, I want him arrested for kidnapping! Right now! I did not permit him to take my baby!! He did not tell me he was taking her! Arrest him! Arrest him now!"

Not once had Shirley made a move to come into the room for little Angel. Instead, she pushed for the police to arrest her father, and they did. They charged him with kidnapping, explaining that he did not have a legal right to take the baby without permission. Mr. Harris never spoke a word and was cooperative enough that the police did not put the cuffs on him! Mrs. Harris stopped talking as well and only asked where they would take her husband.

Shirley, feeling satisfied, then turned to her mother and asked where Angel was because she was taking her and leaving! That is when the female officer took Shirley by the arm and told her she was also under arrest for attempted battery and child endangerment! Two people were arrested for foolishness caused by the heroin that Shirley was addicted to!

Shirley was going to resist when the male officer shot her a look that said he would certainly deal with her if she did! So, to the police station, they went. Mrs. Harris came to the room and asked me if I was alright. I looked back and said, "Are you alright? I and this baby are just fine! I've changed her and she's about ready to eat. I got this baby; you go do what you need to do."

Mrs. Harris and I packed some things for Angel, and I took her home with me. I called my daughter to come by so we could enjoy Angel together and to make sure that if there was trouble, I would not be alone.

Mrs. Harris called her children to tell them what happened, and before you knew it, they were all at the police station to get their husband and father out of jail.

While they were there, one of them inquired about Shirley. She was still there. When she got the chance to make a call, she called her mother's cell phone. Mrs. Harris had decided that she was not answering the phone and gave it to her son instead. He answered and listened to Shirley try to explain her position and how she was not doing anything wrong, and she continued that she was at a friend's house sleeping when her father took Angel. She kept talking, and after a few moments, her brother hung up on her. They left Shirley there.

Social Services came to take a report, and the photo that Mr. Harris took got his charges dropped and solidified a case against Shirley, causing her to lose custody of Angel. The state wanted to put her in foster care until they could be assured that Shirley would not be allowed into the Harris' home.

Shirley was very sick while in jail. The withdrawal was rough, and she had to be hospitalized twice while facing trial for child endangerment. When the public defender was able to get her released, Shirley came straight to the Harris' house. By then, the family installed a door camera. Each time when they saw it was Shirley, they told her to go to a shelter, and she could not come there anymore. She yelled and yelled to see little Angel, but it did not work. At one point, her brother, who had access to the camera, called the police. She had to be warned not to return or be arrested the next time.

Shirley had come to my house after that. She seemed high, but I ignored that hoping I could reach the young lady I knew from long before. We sat outside on the porch. I locked my door as I came out just in case she was up to something.

We talked about a lot of old things at first. I remembered her as a sweet young lady, with a bright future. Now, she is sitting here having made so many bad decisions. Sadly, she is trying to manipulate me to get in on her side. I saw it coming. I was wondering what she will ask for, money or a place to stay.

Then she asked me to help her see her baby. I listened to her explain that she had to have her father arrested for taking her baby, her Angel because he had no right to. I listened to her as she went on about her addiction and how her parents were part of the problem by providing her with money and then not stopping her when she stole items from the house. She took no blame for anything she did or for anything that happened.

When she finished talking, I asked her if she was hungry. She became irritated, but tried to remain in control, and told me no. I rang my doorbell. A moment later, my daughter came out. I turned to Shirley and told her I would help her see her daughter. Shirley jumped up as if we were going right then!

I put my hands up and said, "I will need a moment." I went just inside the house and called the Harris home.

I explained what just happened, and they agreed to let Shirley see Angel using FaceTime.

When I came out and gave Shirley my phone, she was puzzled until she looked down and saw little Angel, sleeping in her crib. Shirley was happy and called her baby several times trying to wake her up. In the next moment, Shirley demanded to know who was holding the phone, and they better let her in if she came back to see Angel. The phone went silent. I put my hand out for my phone, and Shirley threw it onto the porch. My daughter got up, retrieved the phone, and put it in her pocket. She did not sit back down.

There was silence with the three of us just standing there. I believe I was waiting for Shirley to say something, anything. My daughter was waiting for Shirley to do something.

Shirley let out a sigh and looked at us asking what she should do now. She wanted to see her baby in person.

My daughter spoke up saying, "Shirley, you need help. That help must include intense drug rehabilitation. You are going to go to jail without it. You have a beautiful daughter; do it so that you can be a family. We will continue praying for your recovery, your complete recovery! Now, I need to take Mommy inside. If you need a place to stay, I can take you to the shelter. It's still early, and there may still be beds."

Shirley looked at me and asked me to stay the night. My daughter told her no because she was still using. Shirley got angry and stormed off.

Three weeks later, we received news that Shirley was found deceased in that same drug house her father found her. I should not blame myself, but I wondered if I let her stay that night, would she be alive today?

My daughter disagrees. She reminded me that Shirley was on something the last time we saw her. She might have robbed me blind had we let her stay.

The Harris' held a private funeral for Shirley. I kept the baby while they made arrangements. Her siblings took it hard.

Little Angel started walking the day they buried Shirley. The family was so excited about that! Shirley's parents took custody of Angel with the help of her aunts and uncles. The village raised Angel to be a bright, well-rounded, and beautiful young lady. She graduated college; she is engaged, and today, she is a lead news anchor in the area! I watch her every day!

9

Ms. Billie

Now, this lady I am going to tell you about is something else! Most of us have seen movies where people survive the craziest accidents. Well, Billie is one of those people. She is our Forest Gump!

Before Billie was born, a doctor told her mother that the baby she was carrying would not make it. It had something to do with her not growing fast enough inside her momma. When the time came for Billie to be born, they had to go in and get her! She was so fat that when Billie's mother went into labor, 4 hours of pushing and pushing, they had to cut her open! When they weighed Billie, she was sitting just below ten pounds!

When Billie's daddy looked and saw that big baby naked and crying on his wife's belly, he just knew it was a boy! So, he called the baby Billie! When he came to himself, he realized he had a baby girl and decided, so what! He would bust up anyone who teased his baby about her name!

Billie was always a nosey baby. She would lean almost out of the arms of whoever held her to see who came in the door or what the noise was in the other room! She learned to walk early which did not help matters at all! She would walk everywhere there was a sound or a door open. One day, she walked out the front door and fell into a flooded ditch! The way they ran to the ditch when they realized she was not with anyone outside! When her daddy pulled her from the water, he hollered so that everyone thought he would die right there. Luckily, someone knew how to do that resuscitation, and Billie coughed until she started crying. From then on, no one let Billie out of their sight!

Billie was a sharp child! She learned fast, but her curiosity was always just a little on the edge! When she was in elementary school, she wanted to make a bell ring as she saw in school science class. Well, they made that bell ring with electricity! She went and got some wires and rigged them to a socket, thinking she could make a doorbell for her parents. When she stuck that wire in the socket, the electricity sent her flying across the room! Her mother and father came running when they saw the light flicker and found Billie lying on the floor! Her father was just screaming and grabbing for Billie! Billie's momma was the calmer type, but this time, she was shaking. Billie opened her eyes after a short moment and smiled. When they asked her what happened, and Billie explained, her father started laughing! Then Billie started laughing. Billie's momma was not laughing but began to cry with relief that her daughter was alive but too curious!

When Billie graduated high school, she went off to college. She wanted to study anything and everything but settled on engineering. During Spring break one year, she had the chance to go to Thailand with a classmate. Wouldn't you know, one tsunami hit the area where Billie and her friend were staying! Billie was missing for almost four days until her father said something about him calling and calling Billie on her cell phone. The phone seemed to be on because it would not go straight to voicemail. Someone at the American Consulate had an idea, and they activated one of those "find my phone" searches. When I tell you that is how they found Billie! Before she went to Thailand, Billie bought one of those plastic phone envelope things. It is supposed to keep your phone dry if you go swimming. Let me tell you it worked in a tsunami!

When they pinpointed the phone's location and went there, it was still around Billie's neck! She was stuck just under a pile of debris barely hydrated with a broken arm and pelvis! Her friend was also found, safe but with two broken legs and also in need of water! That company received so much business after that story broke! Billie was the face of that company too for a long time!

Today, Billie is married, works for General Electric, and

expecting her first baby. I am praying they don't end up with another Billie!

———

Thank You

I would like to thank God for all His grace and mercy! Thank you to my parents (Micki and James) for loving me unconditionally. Thank you to my father-in-law (Junior) for his support and candor whenever we just sit and talk. Thank you to my sister (Simona), and my real first cousins whose love and fellowship make me thankful that they are there. Thank you to every true friend who helped to keep me in check in some way or another as I went through the process. Thank you to my wonderful children (Jared and Mya).

Thank you, Alice B., Kat B. and Kimberly S. who were my beta readers and kept it real!

Thank you to my editor/publisher for giving me this great chance at a new career!

Lastly, the biggest "thank you" goes to my husband,

James A. You have been there for it all and have helped me to do better and grow professionally and personally. My heart belongs to you, and my love for you is eternal!

To everyone who reads my stories, thank you for the encouragement and support! You rock!

www.ingramcontent.com/pod-product-compliance
Lightning Source LLC
Chambersburg PA
CBHW061334140726
47997CB00003B/988